How do flowers talk to animals?

Written by Jillian Powell

Illustrated by Adrienn Greta Schönberg

Collins

What's in this book?

Listen and say

head

eyes

nose

mouth

Download the audio at www.collins.co.uk/839677

neck

beak

body

hand

Lucy and Dad were in the garden.
"Look at the bees on this flower,"
said Lucy.

The bees love these flowers!

seed

nectar

4

"They're drinking the nectar from the flowers. The flowers invite them," said Dad.

"How do flowers talk to animals, and why?" asked Lucy.

pollen

Plants make pollen. Plants can't move, but bees can carry pollen from flower to flower. Then the plants can make new seeds.

Flowers don't talk, but many flowers have a nice smell. Bees like this smell. They look for the flowers with the best smell.
They drink nectar from flowers.

nectar

pollen

Colour can invite bees, too.
Blue, purple, white and yellow are bees'
favourite colours.

Bees' eyes are different from people's eyes.
Bees can see blue patterns on flowers.
The patterns invite the bees to the flowers.
Our eyes cannot see these blue patterns.

blue patterns

Bees can't see the colour red, but butterflies can. Butterflies look for flowers, too. Their favourite colours are red, orange, purple, pink and white.

butterfly

Some flowers have a strong smell at night. The smell invites some bats to the flowers. The bats get pollen on their bodies and carry the pollen from flower to flower.

bats

Some bats like bad smells! These flowers smell of old fruit. The bats get the pollen on their bodies when they drink nectar from the flowers.

Moths look for flowers at night, too. They like white flowers with a nice smell. They know these flowers have lots of nectar. The moths take the pollen from flower to flower.

moths

Big open flowers invite beetles. They climb into the flower. Beetles' favourite flowers are white and green.

beetle

Short plants with small flowers invite ants. The ants climb up the plants into the flowers. Their bodies pick up the pollen.

ants

These long, red flowers invite hummingbirds. The birds drink the nectar and pick up pollen on their long beaks. The birds take the pollen from flower to flower.

hummingbird

Parrots love the red and pink flowers on these trees. They know they have lots of nectar. The parrots pick up pollen on their heads and necks and take it from flower to flower.

parrot

The big heads of these flowers invite
this small possum. They have lots of
nice nectar. The animals pick up the pollen
on their heads and bodies.

possum

The flowers on these trees have lots of nectar. These lizards climb the tall trees to find the nectar. They pick up the flowers' pollen on their bodies, too.

lizard

Some flowers invite bigger animals.
This lemur opens flowers with its hands.
It moves pollen between flowers on its
hands, nose and mouth.

lemur

We can grow flowers and help many animals. Flowers use colour, smell and food to talk to animals. Animals help plants, too. They take the pollen from flower to flower. This helps more flowers to grow.

That is why flowers talk to animals!

Picture dictionary

Listen and repeat

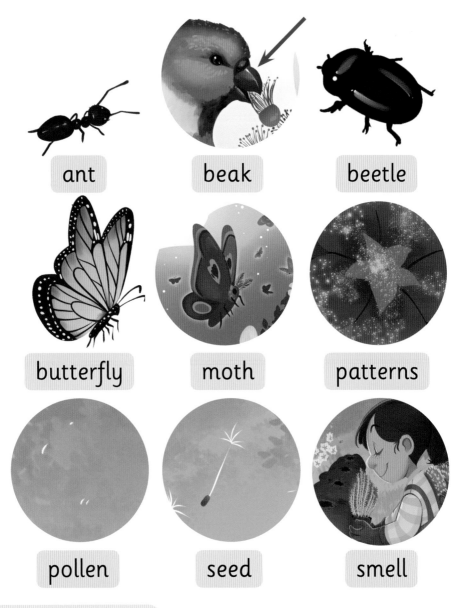

ant

beak

beetle

butterfly

moth

patterns

pollen

seed

smell

After reading

1 Look and match

2 Listen and say

Collins

Published by Collins
An imprint of HarperCollins*Publishers*
Westerhill Road
Bishopbriggs
Glasgow
G64 2QT

HarperCollins*Publishers*
1st Floor, Watermarque Building
Ringsend Road
Dublin 4
Ireland

William Collins' dream of knowledge for all began with the publication of his first book in 1819.

A self-educated mill worker, he not only enriched millions of lives, but also founded a flourishing publishing house. Today, staying true to this spirit, Collins books are packed with inspiration, innovation and practical expertise. They place you at the centre of a world of possibility and give you exactly what you need to explore it.

© HarperCollins*Publishers* Limited 2020

10 9 8 7 6 5 4 3 2

ISBN 978-0-00-839677-0

www.collins.co.uk/elt

British Library Cataloguing in Publication Data

A catalogue record for this publication is available from the British Library.

Author: Jillian Powell
Illustrator: Adrienn Greta Schönberg (Beehive)
Series editor: Rebecca Adlard
Commissioning editor: Zoë Clarke
Publishing manager: Lisa Todd
Product managers: Jennifer Hall and Caroline Green
In-house editor: Alma Puts Keren
Project manager: Emily Hooton
Editor: Matthew Hancock
Proofreaders: Natalie Murray and Michael Lamb
Cover designer: Kevin Robbins
Typesetter: 2Hoots Publishing Services Ltd
Audio produced by id audio, London
Reading guide author: Emma Wilkinson
Production controller: Rachel Weaver
Printed and bound by: GPS Group, Slovenia

MIX
Paper from
responsible sources
FSC
www.fsc.org
FSC™ C007454

This book is produced from independently certified FSC™ paper to ensure responsible forest management.

For more information visit: **www.harpercollins.co.uk/green**

Download the audio for this book and a reading guide for parents and teachers at www.collins.co.uk/839677